2 Xc 4 My Shirt

D0088544

2 Xc 4 My Shirt

Robin and Chris Lawrie

Illustrated by
Robin Lawrie

Acknowledgements

The authors and publishers would like to thank
Julia Francis, Hereford Diocesan Deaf Church
lay co-chaplain, for her help with the sign language
in the *Chain Gang* books.

Published by Evans Brothers Limited
2A Portman Mansions
Chiltern Street
London W1U 6NR

First published 2001

The authors assert their moral right to be identified as the
authors of this work in accordance with the Copyright, Designs
and Patents Act, 1988.

Printed in Hong Kong

British Library Cataloguing in Publication data.
Lawrie, Robin
  2 Xc 4 my shirt. – (The Chain Gang)
  1. Slam Duncan (Fictitious character) – Juvenile fiction
  2. All terrain cycling – Juvenile fiction 3. Adventure stories
  4. Children's stories
  I. Title II. Lawrie, Chris
  823.9'14[J]

ISBN 0 237 52260 8

Hi, my name is "Slam" Duncan. I ride and race mountain bikes with a group of kids called The Chain Gang. There's my best mate and computer ace, Aziz "Dozy" Parmar. There's Fionn, who rides horses as well as bikes. And there's Larry, who is very accident prone, but a good rider. Our best rider is Andy, who is deaf and uses sign language.

This winter there's going to be a series of races to encourage good sportsmanship among young riders. It is called the Sword in the Stump Challenge. There will be two cross-country, two duel descender and two downhill races.

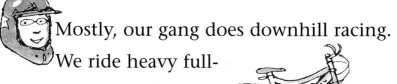

Mostly, our gang does downhill racing. We ride heavy full-suspension bikes which weigh about 15 kg. That's not a problem for going downhill on a one-mile course. But for cross-country racing that's a lot of weight to pedal for 12 miles or more. I planned to get a secondhand, lightweight frame and swop all my kit over to it, except the shocks.

I earn money for biking by working in my dad's garage. But . . .

Sorry, Slam, business is bad. You'll have to find another job. But you can make me a cuppa tea.

You just sacked me! Make your own!

Nothing for it but to get a morning
paper round.

It was a long round.

A 5 a.m. start; cold, wet,
dark and miserable.
The worst part
was that I still
had to go to school at 9 a.m.

YOU! DUNCAN! WAKE UP!

ZZZZZ

But the best part was . . .

. . . riding up
hills was really
getting me fit.

Sometimes I would ride past the
Tuer Health Club, owned by the father
of my arch rival, "Punk" Tuer.

Punk and his mate, "Dyno" Sawyer, were also getting in some early morning training. It was nowhere near as good as real road training, but it looked a lot more fun.

weights

treadmill

At least Miss Soames, at High Top Farm, always had a cup of tea and a biscuit for me at the end of the long climb up to her place.

Puff, puff, wheeze, gasp!

dumbbells

9

I was the only person she saw all day,
so she had lots to say – but the biscuits
were worth it.

... and would you believe it, the price of lambs at the market... it's not worth my while to ... and so I told her, look here, she's no better than she...

HARROW GARAGE
TEL. 341926

Meanwhile, business was still bad at
Dad's garage, and a week before
the race . . .

Sorry, Slam, you'll have to find your own entry fee for this race.

I couldn't afford a frame
as well as the entry fee.
I was stuck. Then, the morning
before the race, I got lucky.

It was rusty and bashed, but
I could pick it up with one finger.

It would do!

11

That night, swapping parts from one frame to another, I wasn't so sure.

The threads on the bottom bracket were stripped and one of the chain stays was cracked. Things looked bad.

I thought Dad would tell me off
for swearing, but he didn't
say anything.

He just got out

his welding torch and

thread cutters and got to work.

The bike still
looked as if it came from a skip
but it rode well, even without shocks.

I fished my racing shirt out

of the bin and washed it,

ready for the race

in the morning.

13

Next day, we met up an hour before the start of the race. Although we knew the course well, and had trained hard, this was our first ever Xc race. We were nervous. The lads in our gang were unlikely to win against real cross-country riders, but we could score precious points towards the "Challenge". Fionn, however, could win the girls' race.

10 a.m. We were off! Twelve miles of hard cross-country racing. The course started with a tough uphill climb to space out the 40 riders. Dozy, Larry, and Andy were going for it, and even on their downhill bikes had shot ahead. I was pacing myself but was still well up in the pack and staying ahead of Punk and Dyno.

Pant! Gasp!

Puff! Puff!

Puff! Wheeze!

eXcalibur START-FINISH

My bike had no shock absorbers to sap my climbing power. And my early morning training was paying off.

16

Then Dozy
hit a muddy patch.

His slick racing tyres started to slip and he
crashed heavily. I stopped to help him . . .

17

. . . but there was nothing I could do. With the wrong tyres, his race was finished.

Then, on the stony descent off the hill, my rigid forks really slowed me down. Punk and Dyno, with front shocks, shot past me.

I rattled round the next bend, straight into the back of Larry standing at the edge of a major dropoff. He looked grey!

Again, there was nothing I could do.

I took the drop
at top speed, hoping
that no-one else had made
a mess of things. No such luck.

At the bottom of the hill I found Andy.
He hadn't heard the rider
behind him shouting
that he wanted
to overtake.

Andy had been forced into the trees and
bent a wheel. He signed:

There was nothing I could do.

1. No good! 2. I'm a 3. danger to others.

I caught Punk and Dyno on the next long climb. Dyno was done for. I overtook Punk at the top, and started belting down the other side when suddenly . . .

. . . the course was full of Sam Jones's sheep. They had come through a gate someone had left open.

I had to stop and help him to round them up.

21

. . . the marshall for that section must have been asleep because there were horse riders entering the course.

I knew that horses panicked when you sneaked up on them so I slowed and let them know I was there. However, there is someone who never slows down for ANYTHING!

The horses went BALLISTIC!

I didn't
know what to do.
But as luck would
have it . . .

. . . Fionn, who knows all about horses, had caught me up.

She helped me to calm them down. The other girl bikers streamed past. As downhillers, the best we lads were hoping for in an Xc race was a few championship points.

Fionn, however, had been on course for a win in girls. She was GUTTED!

I had to get back to chasing Punk.
By this time
I was covered
in mud and completely
fed up. But his stupid, dangerous riding
was no substitute for fitness. On the next
climb, I started reeling
him in again.

Puff, puff,
Wheeze!

I overtook him at the top.

Puff. Choke. Wheeze!

This time I was going to make it stick . . . even downhill!

NO MORE MR NICE GUY, no matter who needed my help. But then . . .

Oh, Slam, I'm so glad to see you! Jenny, the new calf, has run off and I've got myself stuck on this stile. I don't know what to do. You haven't got a minute, have you?

What should I do?
I thought about King Arthur
and his sword, Excalibur.
He and his Knights of
the Round Table
would never,
ever let down
a friend
or fail to
rescue a damsel in distress.
Maybe this was the real challenge
of the Sword in the Stump.

SHARING

Punk got a 6th
and 95 points.
I scored zero, just like
the rest of the gang.

29

Next day, I had a look at some mega-pricey cross-country shock absorbers in the window of Tuer Cycles. Nice forks, shame about the price.

I was telling Dad all about them later when Sam Jones, the sheep farmer, drove into the yard.

Ten minutes later . . .

Five minutes after that . . .

It's Miss Soames!

I was just driving along and all of a sudden I heard this funny noise, a bit like a cow giving birth. Oh dear, I said to myself, that sounds very expensive, what shall I do? Then I remembered seeing the name of a garage on the back of Slam's shirt. What was it called—The Plough, no. The Furrow, no. The . . . . .

Some time later . . .

. . . the Harrow, that was it!

Much, much later . . .

Brilliant, Slam, you're a real knight in shining armour. There's lots of work here.

It was nothing, Dad, I guess I'm just too Xc for my shirt.

Ah, yes, maybe some bike improvements are called for.

But, two days later . . .